A HOUSE
by the RIVER

by WILLIAM MILLER

illustrated by

CORNELIUS VAN WRIGHT *and* YING-HWA HU

LEE & LOW BOOKS INC. • *New York*

Text copyright © 1997 by William Miller
Illustrations copyright © 1997 by Cornelius Van Wright and Ying-Hwa Hu
All rights reserved. No part of this book may be reproduced, transmitted, or
stored in an information retrieval system in any form or by any means, electronic,
mechanical, photocopying, recording, or otherwise, without written permission
from the publisher.
LEE & LOW BOOKS Inc., 95 Madison Avenue, New York, NY 10016
leeandlow.com

Book design by Christy Hale
Book production by The Kids at Our House

The text is set in Giovanni Book
The illustrations are rendered in watercolor

Manufactured in China by RR Donnelley Limited, March 2016
(hc) 10 9 8 7 6 5 4 3 2 1
(pb) 10 9 8 7 6 5 4 3 2 1
First Edition

Library of Congress Cataloging-in-Publication Data
Miller, William
A house by the river/by William Miller; illustrated by Cornelius Van Wright
and Ying-Hwa Hu.—1st ed.
p.   cm.
Summary: Belinda's courage is tested when she and her mother sit out a storm,
hoping that their house will protect them from the rising river.
ISBN 978-1-880000-48-9 (hardcover) ISBN 978-1-62014-305-6 (paperback)
[1. Mothers and daughters—Fiction. 2. Storms—Fiction. 3. Dwellings—Fiction.
4. Courage—Fiction. 5. Afro-Americans—Fiction.] I. Van Wright, Cornelius, ill.
II. Hu, Ying-Hwa, ill. III. Title.
PZ7.M63915Ho 1997
[E]—dc20   96-24137   CIP AC

Belinda didn't like her house by the river. It was small, and the yard was only a patch of dirt.

Her mother raised chickens and pigs that sometimes wandered too far from the yard. It was Belinda's job to drive them back with a stick. She chased and shouted, picking her way through the mud.

But the job she hated most was gathering the eggs. Because she was small, Belinda had to crawl beneath the house, all the way to the dark corners where the chickens liked to roost.

At least once a year, the river threatened the lowland around their house. Swollen by the spring rains, it pounded angrily against the flood wall.

Many times Belinda wondered why they lived so close to the river, why they didn't move to town where the houses were built on hilltops. Her mother always told her that their house was special; special because it was theirs.

But when she rode the bus to school, Belinda envied the other kids, their safe, dry homes without a single pig in the yard.

One morning, as she was getting dressed for school, Belinda smelled the rain in the air. The sky outside her window was low and dark. The rumble of thunder rolled down the river road.

The first heavy drops fell before she reached the yard. While they fell, while the dirt turned quickly to mud, Belinda filled the pigs' trough with corn.

Thunder split the sky overhead, and the pigs squealed, refusing to eat.

Her mother had gone to town for cornmeal and matches for the fire. Belinda was worried that the river would rise and rise. How would her mother make it back?

Belinda had never felt so alone. She had never hated the
house, the dirt and the river as much as she did now.

The school bus would probably not come. On stormy days,
the driver turned back, afraid the bus would get stuck in the mud,
stranding the other children far from their homes.

Belinda wished the bus would come, that she would have to
stay in town, on the high hilltops with one of her girlfriends.
Safe, dry, sitting beside a fire, they would comb their dolls' hair,
while the river rose somewhere far below them....

The storm got worse, and Belinda saw only the lights of her mother's truck as she turned into the yard.

With a sack in her arms, Belinda's mother jumped from one flat rock to the next. "Rain rocks," her mother called them, the only way to save their shoes.

"No school today," she said, putting the sack down. "This could be the worst storm we've had in ten years. At least that's what the gas station man said." Her mother's clothes were drenched, and Belinda could see she was shivering.

Inside, Belinda wrapped a blanket around their shoulders. They sat together listening to the storm. The fire popped and hissed when rain trickled down the narrow chimney.

"Why can't we move, Mama?" Belinda asked. "Why can't we rent one of those houses in town?"

Her mother held her tightly.

"You might not believe it, baby girl, but this place once looked like heaven on earth to your daddy and me. We worked up north in the factories for years, just so we could have a place of our own. A house by the river."

Belinda didn't remember her dad. He died in a car accident not long after she was born.

"The very first night we slept here, we didn't even have wood for the fire. And when we woke up in the morning there was snow all over the blankets, all over the floor."

"Snow?" Belinda asked, giving her mother a puzzled look.

"That's right. This house was in a lot worse shape then than it is now. In fact, we found some little rabbit tracks in all that snow."

Belinda sat up. "Rabbit tracks? How did a rabbit get in here?"

"Nothing to keep them out if they had a mind to come inside. But we were glad to see those tracks. Rabbits are good luck for young married folks. They mean you're going to have a baby before long. At least that's what the old people used to say."

Belinda was thinking about the snow and the tracks so hard, she almost forgot about the storm.

"It's time for the buckets," her mother said. The wind shook the house, and they could hear the steady drip of rain in the next room.

Belinda held the lamp high, while her mother placed buckets on the floor. The soft light fell on an old picture.

"What was his name?" Belinda asked. She knew she was somehow related to the proud, old man.

"That was your great-grandfather, Elias," her mother said. "He was born way back in slavery times. But his children were free people, born after the war."

The wind moaned around the corners of the house. They soon ran out of buckets and pans to catch the rain.

"We'd better go on up, baby girl," her mother said, smiling bravely. "This old storm's about to do his worst." Belinda felt her stomach tighten. They only went to the loft when a storm was really bad. It had been years since Belinda had climbed the shaky ladder.

A small window let them see as far as the river bank. Between gusts of rain, they saw huge tree branches, and tin roofs of old barns swept along by the terrible current.

"Everything's going to be all right," her mother said. "As long as we sit tight, this old house won't fail us."

Belinda wasn't so sure. They stood at the window, her mother holding her tightly once more.

"You were born up here," she whispered. "Your daddy held you up to this very window. He thanked the moon and stars for his daughter, then he pressed your hand against the glass."

Belinda closed her eyes and wished her father was there now. It seemed that every time the wind blew, the old wood creaked louder, came closer to breaking into a thousand pieces.

"Blow on, storm," her mother said. "You can't take what's ours."

"Blow on," Belinda whispered, feeling the house fight back, protecting her like a mother and father....

The next morning, the house was still standing, just like her mother said it would. Together they looked out the window and saw that the rain had stopped in time. The river had just begun to top the flood wall.

When Belinda finally walked outside,
she was never so glad to see her muddy yard. Some
of the pigs had even found their way back, and
were romping in the fresh, brown mud.

A few fat hens pecked around the porch, as if
this was just another day, as if the storm had
never happened.

Belinda remembered her mother's story, the story of their house, and crawled beneath the porch.

Digging carefully in the mud, she felt something round, breakable. She carried it back to the house, back to her mother: a single egg without a crack, stronger than the storm.